First published in the United States, Great Britain, Canada,
Australia, and New Zealand in 2001 by North-South Books,
an imprint of Nord-Süd Verlag AG, Gossau Zürich, Switzerland.
Distributed in the United States by North-South Books Inc., New York.
Library of Congress Cataloging-in-Publication Data is available.
A CIP catalogue record for this book is available from The British Library.
ISBN 0-7358-1501-1 (trade binding) 10 9 8 7 6 5 4 3 2 1
ISBN 0-7358-1502-X (library binding) 10 9 8 7 6 5 4 3 2 1
Printed in Germany
For more information about our books, and the authors and artists
who create them, visit our web site: www.northsouth.com

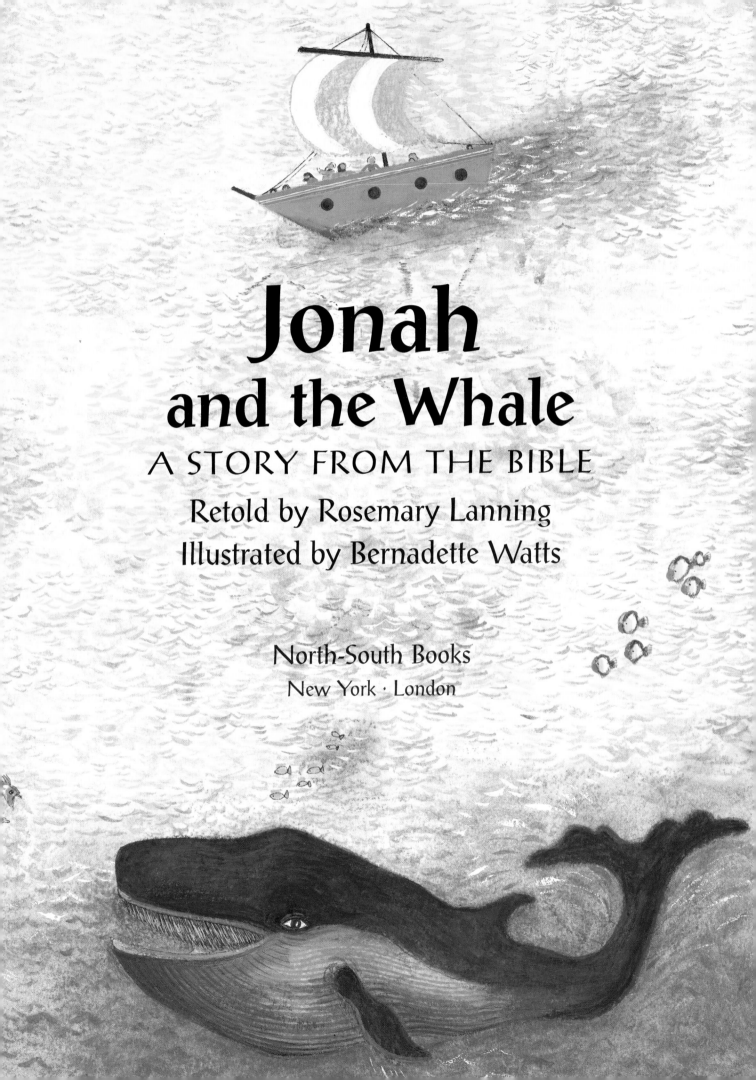

Jonah
and the Whale
A STORY FROM THE BIBLE

Retold by Rosemary Lanning

Illustrated by Bernadette Watts

North-South Books

New York · London

Long, long ago there lived a man named Jonah.
One day Jonah heard the voice of God, saying, "Go to
the city of Nineveh. The people there have grown greedy
and vain. Tell them to change their ways."

Jonah did not want to go to Nineveh. Why me? he thought. Nineveh is no concern of mine.

So he ran away and boarded a ship bound for Tarshish, far across the sea, where God would not find him.

But God sent a mighty wind to stir up the sea.
The little ship was tossed and battered by huge
waves. It would surely break up and sink if the
storm did not pass.

The sailors were terrified. First they prayed to their gods.
Then they threw things overboard to make the ship lighter,
but it was no use. They called Jonah to come and help them.

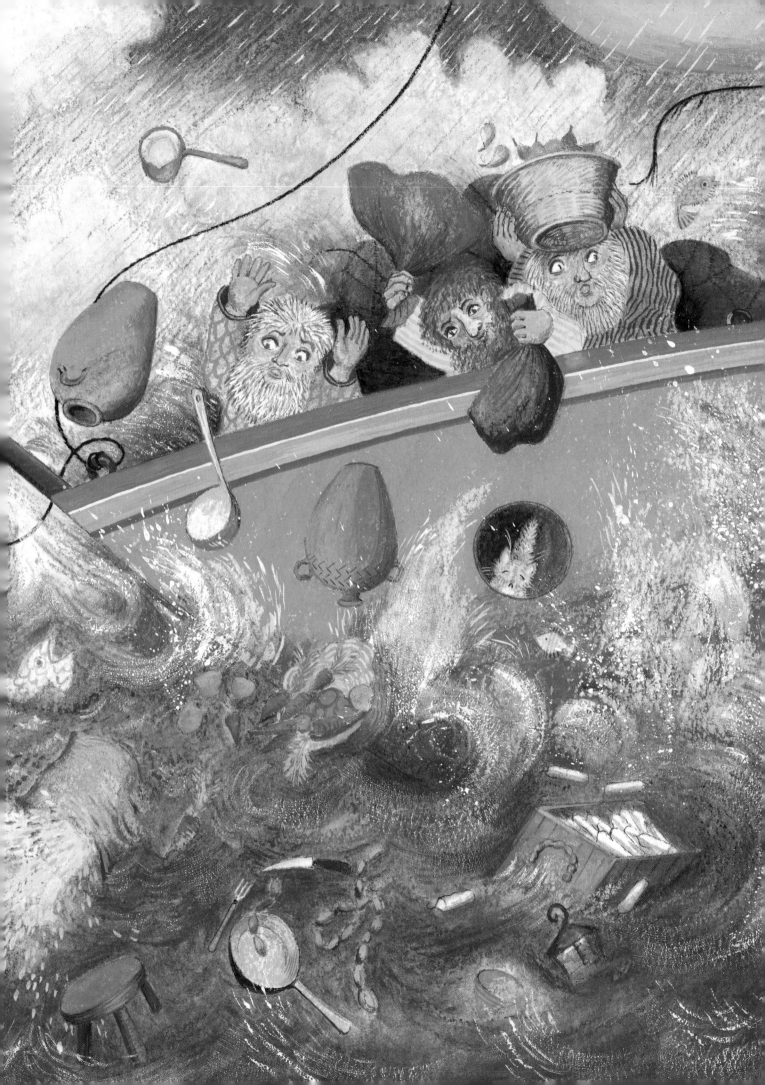

Jonah did not hear. He was fast asleep in the cabin. "How can you sleep in this storm?" cried the captain. "Our ship is going to sink! Come up on deck and pray to your God. Perhaps he can save us!"

The sailors said, "Someone on this ship must have done
something terrible to bring us such bad luck."
"It is me," said Jonah. "I am running away from God. Throw
me overboard and the storm will die down."
The sailors tried to row the ship back to port, so that Jonah
could go ashore, but the storm grew even fiercer and drove
them back. So they had to throw Jonah overboard. At once
the sea was calm again.

God sent a whale to swallow Jonah.
For three days and three nights Jonah lived in the belly
of the whale. He prayed, and thanked God for saving him:
"You were angry with me, O Lord, but you rescued me.
I will do whatever you ask now."

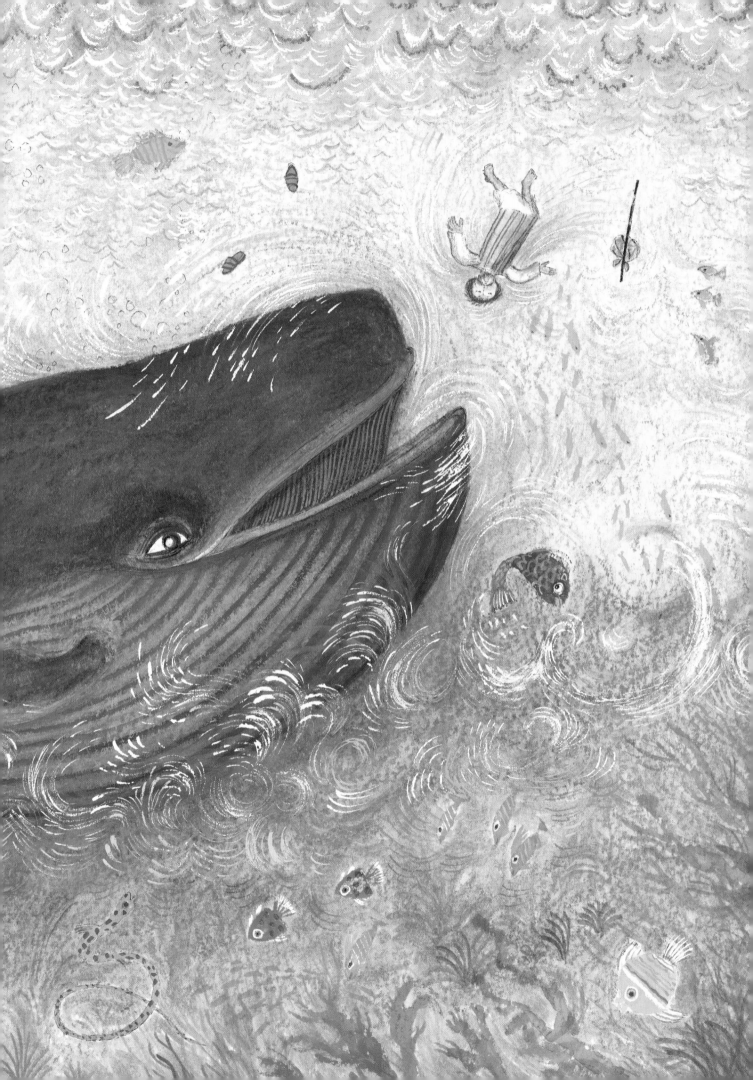

God heard his prayer, and told the whale to spit
Jonah out onto dry land.

Now Jonah made his way to Nineveh as God had commanded.

He stood in the marketplace and told the people:
"God has sent me to say that your city will be destroyed
in forty days!"

The people of Nineveh believed him. When their king
heard what Jonah said, he took off his fine robes and
dressed in rough sackcloth. He ordered his people to do
the same, and to beg God to spare them.

God was pleased that the people of Nineveh had changed their ways. And when forty days passed, he did nothing to harm them. The city of Nineveh was saved.